THE
Fearless
FANTABULOUS FIVE

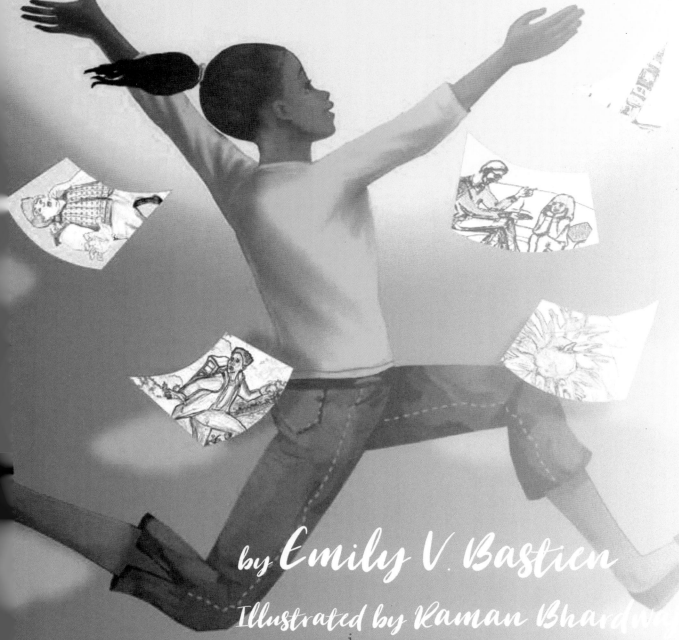

by Emily V. Bastien

Illustrated by Raman Bhardwaj

i

The Fearless Fantabulous Five is a collection of five original short stories. The stories share a common message of courage, hope, and faith. They remind us that during times of trouble, praying and trusting God is the best way to go from fearful to fearless. This book is dedicated to everyone living in fear and wondering how to escape it.

A life of fearlessness is fantabulous!

Table of Contents

Special thanks to my fans who supported my first book, Aqua Tales, and continue to share in my journey as an author. I pray you like this new book.

To my friends and family, thank you!

LONDON RESCUE

Europe Anyone? My family and I went on a European vacation, which included a trip to London. It was delightful to see all the British sites. We went to Buckingham Palace where Queen Elizabeth lives and peeked through the gates.

We watched the Changing of the Guards. There were five guards wearing the same black uniform with yellow and red tassels. Two guards stood at attention while three marched in rhythm and switched position with them effortlessly.

We also visited the Princess Diana Memorial Playground in the renowned Kensington Gardens, and spent hours there playing with other kids. I really enjoyed the London Natural History Museum with its moving dinosaurs and outer space exhibits.

At the Langham Hotel, we enjoyed a traditional British Afternoon Tea with crumpets, sandwiches cut in the shape of animals, and tiny delicious cakes. This was a special treat for my sister's birthday, but I ate most of the cakes.

Exploring all the London sites was wonderful, I enjoyed every moment of it until the very last night. On the last night before we returned home, we were at my great grandma's house. My sister, Elise, was chasing me around the house. I ran into my great grandma's upstairs bedroom and quickly locked the door behind me.

Can you find the FIVE hidden objects in this picture?

I thought I was safe until I tried to open the door. I could not. Elise ran to the door and was telling me to "let her in." Through the door I yelled, "Go tell mommy that I am stuck inside the bedroom." I could hear her footsteps as she ran to get help.

My mother came to door asking, "Emily, are you O.K.?" I was trying to be brave, but hearing her voice made me start crying right away. I was trapped inside my great grandma's bedroom and the door would not open. I could hear Elise saying, "Emily, do not worry and do not cry. I am here and mommy will get you out soon."

My mother, great grandma, and aunt all tried opening the door. They tried a knife, wrench, hammer, and other tools, but the door would not budge at all. Great grandma then told me to pull the key out and slip it under the door. I pulled the key with all my strength. It popped out of the key hole into my hand and I slipped it under the door. From the outside, she jiggled the key in the door.

I started praying that this trick with the key would work. While I was praying, I heard my Aunt Jackie say, "Stand back, I have my heavy boots on and I am about to kick the door down." This made me laugh even though tears were still running down my face. I wish I could have seen my aunt's face as she prepared to kick the door down.

Elise then yelled, "Emily, move away from the door! Auntie Jackie is kicking in the door." I jumped off the bed and quickly ran to the opposite side of the room. I heard two loud thumps. The door shook with each kick, but nothing else happened. I started to get more scared when the door did not budge.

My mom said, "Emily, lay on the bed and watch television while we figure out how to open the door." I decided to pray even harder so I would not be stuck in the room forever. This was not what I imagined when I thought about my last night in London.

It felt like several hours being trapped in that room with no way to escape. Fear started to creep up in my heart and it began to fill the room. Out of nowhere, I heard a man's voice saying, "Emily, stand back." I did not recognize the voice, but I listened to the directions.

Another voice then said, "We will have to remove the door molding and handle." A woman's voice said, "I will go outside to see if we can get through the window." I felt much better knowing there was a plan to save me. I decided I would no longer be afraid and kept on praying, "God, please help me. I want to be rescued from this bedroom."

After about ten minutes, the door was pushed open from the outside. There were two firefighters standing at the door. They were big and tall with bright red shirts, black pants, and black boots. I jumped off the bed, ran passed them to my mom, and gave her a big hug. Everyone was cheering and clapping their hands.

The firefighters – Claire, Tim and Ellie – were kind and friendly. They allowed Elise and me to go onto the fire truck and wear their fire helmets. We also took pictures with them to remember the night I was rescued from London. I went from being fearful to fearless that night.

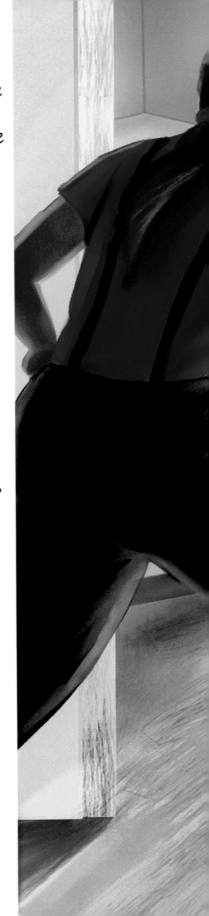

6

GRAPE SEED

There once was a little girl named Lisa. She had long red hair and freckles. She was an only child, but had lots of friends at school. Her four best friends were Beatrice, Molly, Rose, and Tom. Beatrice was into fashion and always wore bright colors. Molly, Beatrice's twin sister, was the most popular girl in school because of her bubbly personality. She often wore yellow, which was her favorite color.

Rose was not as popular as Molly. She was very shy and did not speak much, but she was a good friend to Lisa. Lisa could spot her from far away because of her bright orange backpack. Tom was the only boy in their friendship circle. He was a very good soccer player and could pass for Lisa's brother because of his red hair. Lisa really liked hanging out with her school friends. They shared everything from lunch and laughs to secrets and stories.

When Lisa decided to become a Christian, she was very excited to tell her friends and all her classmates. They started asking her many questions about the Bible, but Lisa could not answer all the questions. Her classmates and her friends began laughing and pointing at her. "You cannot be a Christian if you do not know the Bible. You are NOT a real Christian." She did not understand why her friends were being so mean to her. Their reaction really hurt her feelings. Lisa walked away while her friends were teasing her. She left school and went home very sad.

Lisa's dad tried to cheer her up when she got home, but nothing made her feel better. As she sat sadly on the sofa, Lisa's dad joined her. He said, "I am going to tell you a story. Once upon a time, there was a grape seed. It was planted, but it was not growing. The grape seed could not grow by itself; it needed help. It needed water and sunlight to bud and grow.

Over time, the grape seed got all the important things it needed and started to bud. While it was budding inside, no one noticed it. It was changing on the inside, but it looked the same on the outside. A new Christian is just like a grape seed. They are planted in God, but their growth is not always noticed by others right away.

The change inside is noticed when a Christian gets water. Jesus said 'I am the living water.' A Christian also needs 'the Son' which guides them along the path of life. The Son of God shines on Christians to help them during hard times. The Son of God shines through them so others can see His kindness and love. In life, bad things happen to everyone -- even to kids. When these things happen, we can trust in God to help and protect us from Satan.

Satan is always trying to pluck us off the vine or pull us up from the root. This plucking and pulling can destroy a young plant. Like a young plant, Christians have to hold strong as they grow from seeds into mature plants so they can be used by God. God wants to use us for many things, like helping others. A ripe cluster of grapes can also be used for many things. It can be turned into grape juice or put into a fruit salad."

"You see," said dad, "Now, you are just a little seed being planted, but soon you will begin to grow. Once you bud, mature, and turn into a faithful Christian, God will use you to change lives." "O.K.," said Lisa, putting her coat back on with a smile. "I will not let fear stop me. I may not know the answers to my friends' questions, but I know that God loves me. I am going to tell others that God loves them too. This is what real Christians do."

1 Corinthians 3:6–7 says, "I planted the seed, Apollos watered it, but God has been making it grow. So neither the one who plants nor the one who waters is anything, but only God, who makes things grow."

11

TWO TRAILS

Everyone loves having choices. Everyday, most kids get to choose what to do for fun. Some kids like playing sports or listening to music, while others like watching television or reading books. Parents have choices too. They get to choose how late to go to bed. Some parents fall asleep before midnight and others are up way after midnight. It is nice to have lots of choices, but people do not always make the right choice.

Chris was one of these people. Chris, a tall athletic teenager, had to learn the hard way how to make the right choice in life. He learned this lesson on a bright sunny day when he decided to explore the park near his house. The park was often filled with deer, squirrels, birds, and sometimes even rabbits. It also had a beautiful waterfall, which could be seen from miles away. Chris packed his bag with water, snacks, and all the hiking gear he would need for the day. He prepared himself for the best day ever.

Pick out your FIVE favorite things in this park?

Chris got to the park early and headed towards his favorite spot near the Boobala River. The river was so clean you could drink from it. Usually, Chris would swim for hours in the river, but he decided that today he would first explore some trails. Once he started walking along the river, he came upon a fork, which split into two trails. One going to the right and another towards the left. He did not know which trail to take.

As Chris was thinking about which trail to take, he felt a tap on his shoulder. He turned around, but did not see anyone behind him. He heard a voice say, "You should take the left trail towards the waterfall. The path is clear and much wider. Trust me, you will be safe." Chris was thinking about the best choice to make when he felt a second tap on his other shoulder.

Another voice said, "Chris, you should go to the right towards the tall trees. The path may look thorny now, but this is your best choice. Trust me, I will protect you." Chris wondered why the second voice, which sounded like Jesus said, "Take the thorny trail." Chris knew it was Jesus because that voice guided him in the past when he prayed for help. He stood there for awhile thinking about the best choice to make.

Finally, Chris decided to go on the trail towards the waterfall. As far as his eyes could see, it was much clearer and the view was better. He did not believe that the thorny trail towards the tall trees would be the best choice. Chris was confused why Jesus would tell him to take that trail. He did not want to get hurt by thorns. No one wants to be pricked by thorns.

He knew his decision was not what Jesus told him to do, but he wanted to be safe. The trail he chose was perfect in the beginning. He could hear the waterfall while he hiked and he saw all types of animals on his journey. He started smiling to himself because he was very sure he had made the right decision. Everything about his hike was enjoyable until things took a turn for the worst.

When Chris was at the halfway point, he looked around and saw something he had never seen before in his life. The clear trail he was on began to change. There were now rugged rocks, thorns, spiders, and poisonous snakes everywhere. He started to get pricked by thorns and hissed at by snakes.

Chris became terrified by the scene. His heart started beating fast. He was sweating all over and his hands were shaking out of control. He started yelling for help, but there was no one around to help him. After yelling for awhile and hearing no answer, he decided to run. It was very hard to run on the rugged rocks and through the thick thorns. Chris ran for awhile and was soon out of breath.

At that moment, Chris cried out, "Jesus, please help! This trail is dangerous and I am scared." Jesus answered him by saying, "Chris, why did you disobey me at the start of your hiking trip?" Chris replied, "I did not want to get hurt. I did not know that this trail would become filled with thorns and snakes." Jesus replied, "Chris, turn back."

Chris started running again. This time he ran over two miles in the opposite direction towards the fork in the trail. Once he got there, he stopped running and sat on the ground. His legs were bleeding from the thorns, his feet were sore from running, and his back was in pain. He decided to go home instead of going swimming.

After getting home and cleaning himself up, he went straight to bed. The next day, Chris told his family and friends about his hiking adventure and how he learned an important lesson. He learned to listen to Jesus' voice and to always trust Him. Where there is trust, there is no fear.

ESA AND THE FIRST

Esa was a pretty girl. She had soft brown hair and brown eyes. She was the youngest in her family. She was very smart and loved to read. Her favorite book to read was the Bible because it was filled with great stories. At six years old, she learned the Ten Commandments. She would recite them everyday on the way to school. While at school, Esa would read books or play on the playground during recess.

One day, Esa decided to swing on the brand new monkey bars. While swinging, a kid about two feet taller than Esa started yelling at her. He yelled, "What are you doing on my monkey bars?" She kept on swinging. He then said, "If you don't get off, I will pull you off." "What is your name?" Esa asked the kid as he grabbed and twisted her feet. He replied, "My name is Anthony. I am the boss of this school. Now get off my monkey bars!"

Anthony was very mean. He had red hair, a red face, and was taller than the kids in class. Before Esa could say anything else, Anthony pulled her off the monkey bars. Esa did not say a word. She looked at Anthony and then ran away scared with tears in her eyes. All the kids on the playground watched as Esa was being bullied, but none of them helped her.

The next day, Esa decided that she would always obey Anthony. She did not want him to hurt her or make fun of her. Esa started following all his directions instead of doing what was right. As she walked home, she thought to herself, "I had a great day because I listened to Anthony, but I feel sad inside. I know I am listening to the wrong person."

Esa thought about Anthony being mean every day that week. When she went to church, she asked her Sabbath school teacher for help. The teacher reminded her, "The Bible said not to worship idols. There is only one true God." She realized that she was treating Anthony like a god.

She decided she would have to stand up to Anthony. The next school day, Esa went on the monkey bars again. She wanted so badly to swing on the bars, but she was very nervous about upsetting Anthony. She prayed that Anthony would not be at school, but he showed up a few minutes later. He yelled from across the field, "Didn't I tell you to stay off my monkey bars?" Anthony's yelling made him look three times as big as he did before.

Esa started to panic and her knees shook. She silently prayed, "God, please help me." She then jumped off the bars towards him. Esa responded, "Yes, you did tell me to stay off the monkey bars, but I am no longer listening to you. I will not treat you like a god or worship you anymore." "You listen to me," said Anthony. "I am the boss of this school."

Esa pointed to the sky and said, "No. I am supposed to listen to God. I will no longer listen to you. You are not a nice person." Anthony stared at Esa for a very long time. She was not sure what to do, but decided to stand her ground. Everyone on the playground watched in silence. Anthony turned bright red in the face and slowly walked away in shock.

The kids who saw what happened were very surprised and happy. Some of them started cheering and clapping their hands for Esa. They asked her, "How did you have the courage to stand up to him?" Esa shared that in church she learned to only worship the true God. The kids were excited to learn more about God because they saw how He protected Esa. They thought Anthony would have tried to hurt her, but instead he just walked away.

Anthony never bothered Esa again. She became popular because of her bravery. Soon more kids were standing up to Anthony because of Esa's example. Esa was the first to confront him about being a bully. She was the first one willing to share her beliefs without fear of being laughed at by others. She obeyed the first commandment and it made a difference in her school.

FALLEN ROBIN

Elise woke me up early one Sunday morning. I usually do not like it when she wakes me up, but this morning was different. It was going to be a warm and sunny day. We prayed together, washed our faces, brushed our teeth, and then ran downstairs.

We played lots of games together and made up silly songs for our pretend school. Some of the lyrics for our school song are:
"Clap your Hands (tap, tap, tap)
Stomp your Feet (boom, boom, boom)
Touch your Nose then Touch your Toes
Turn Around and Sit Down"

After awhile, we woke our parents up for breakfast. Dad made a yummy breakfast including eggs, pancakes, fruits, and hot chocolate. After breakfast, we ran outside to enjoy the warm weather. We played outside while our mom stayed inside to eat her breakfast and clean up the kitchen.

Dad came outside with us and went to work in the garden. He was removing weeds and watering the flowers while Elise and I were running all over the front yard. We were sliding, swinging, and climbing ropes on our swing set. We were having the best time until we heard Dad say, "Girls, it's time to go back inside."

I was not happy about going inside, but headed towards the house anyway. As I was walking up the steps, I looked over the railing and saw something surprising. At first, I did not know what it was, so I leaned in closer. I saw a furry grayish-brown ball in the grass. I called Elise so she could look at it too. We realized it was not a ball, but a baby robin.

The robin was wet, shivering, and curled in a ball. The little birdie was scared and alone. It was making chirping sounds as it laid on the ground. I told Elise that the hatchling was calling for its mother, but we did not see the mother anywhere around the front yard. We called our dad and showed him the baby robin. He told us not to touch it.

He then went to the garage to get his bright yellow gloves. These were his special gloves for gardening. I was curious to see what he was going to do with them. After putting on his gloves, dad went searching for the robin's nest. It was like he went on an adventure in our front yard. It took him a few minutes to find the nest because it was hidden in the pine tree next to the front door.

The baby robin had fallen very far. The nest was high up in the pine tree and was made of tiny sticks, leaves and paper. After finding the nest, dad came back to where we were hovering over the bird. He gently picked it up with his bright yellow gloves. We then noticed the mother bird watching us from a safe distance.

She had a black head, orange belly, and gray wings. She started chirping very loudly when she saw Dad holding her baby. Dad said, "Girls, you will have to distract the mother so I can get the baby up to the nest safely." The baby robin looked scared as dad carried it back to the nest.

It tried to make itself into a smaller ball. Dad climbed the steps and gently put the hatchling back into the nest. I know the birdie was happy to be safe and free. When it gets bigger, I can imagine it flying fearlessly.

Dad, Elise and I were excited that we saved the baby robin. We ran inside the house, and I told mom right away the story of the rescue. Our mom smiled and gave me a big hug. She told me that God allowed me to go outside to play knowing I would see the hatchling on the ground needing help.

I smile every time I think about helping the baby robin. It reminds me that God will always send someone to help us whenever we are in need. God always rescues us. He also expects us to help others who have fallen down. With God by our side, we can be friendly, fearless, and fantabulous!

The Bible says, "You pushed me violently, that I might fall, but the LORD helped me." (Psalms 118:13)

THE END

HOPE IN TIMES OF FEAR

Are you scared, living in fear and wondering how to escape it? Here are some Bible verses which remind me to trust God when I am scared. I pray they will encourage you and give you hope.

"Be strong and courageous. Do not be afraid or terrified because of them, for the Lord your God goes with you; he will never leave you nor forsake you." ~ Deuteronomy 31:6

"The Lord is my light and my salvation – whom shall I fear? The Lord is the strength of my life – of whom shall I be afraid?" ~ Psalm 27:1

"I prayed to the Lord, and he answered me. He freed me from all my fears." ~ Psalm 34:4

"When I am afraid, I put my trust in you." ~ Psalm 56:3

"The Lord is with me; I will not be afraid. What can man do to me? The Lord is with me; he is my helper." ~ Psalm 118:6-7

"Tell everyone who is discouraged, Be strong and don't be afraid! God is coming to your rescue." ~ Isaiah 35:4

"Therefore do not worry about tomorrow, for tomorrow will worry about itself. Each day has enough trouble of its own."
~ Matthew 6:34

"Peace is what I leave with you; it is my own peace that I give you. I do not give it as the world does. Do not be worried and upset; do not be afraid." ~ John 14:27

"For God has not given us a spirit of fear, but of power and of love and of a sound mind." ~ 2 Timothy 1:7

"But even if you suffer for doing what is right, God will reward you for it. So don't worry or be afraid of their threats."
~ 1 Peter 3:14

"There is no fear in love. But perfect love drives out fear, because fear has to do with punishment. The one who fears is not made perfect in love." ~ 1 John 4:18

"Then he placed his right hand on me and said: 'Do not be afraid. I am the First and the Last.'" ~ Revelation 1:17

Verses from the Bible - New International Version.

ABOUT THE AUTHOR

Emily V. Bastien was one of the youngest published authors in US history when she released her first book – Aqua Tales – at seven years old. Her passion and persistence made her first book a reality. Writing a book at any age is a significant accomplishment, but in an era where one in four American children grows up without learning how to read, Emily, is one of a kind.

Emily is an avid reader who loves to create her own stories. At nine years old, Emily released her second book, The Fearless Fantabulous Five, in November 2018. She proves that age is never an obstacle when kids are determined to achieve their goals. Emily shares her love for reading and writing throughout the United States, Europe and Caribbean Islands.

ABOUT THE ILLUSTRATOR

Raman Bhardwaj was born in Chandigarh, India. As a child, he loved to draw. He has a BFA degree (Applied art) and MA (History of Art) both with merit and UGC eligibility for lectureship in India. He received a National award by N.C.E.R.T (India) for children book illustration in Punjabi language category.

Raman is now a freelance artist who has illustrated many children books for authors all over the world. He created scores of humorous character animations for a leading entertainment site. He also worked as Chief Designer and illustrator for The Times of India in Chandigarh, India. Raman currently resides in Greensboro, NC with his family.

Become a "Fearless Fantabulous Fan," share your comments and review on Amazon.com and Emily's Social Media Pages:

Facebook: www.facebook.com/EmilyVBastien

Instagram: www.instagram.com/EmilyVBastien

Website: www.EmilyVBastien.com

Emily's first book, Aqua Tales, is available on Amazon and Kindle.

Aqua Tales is a collection of short stories about kids solving problems and overcoming life's challenges. It offers creative solutions for children and reinforces the importance of love, trust, and honesty. Aqua Tales provides a unique glimpse into nature through the eyes of a young girl and encourages readers to let their imagination run wild. Whether you are a scaredy hunter or a talk mouth, this book will capture you heart and inspire you to pursue your dreams.

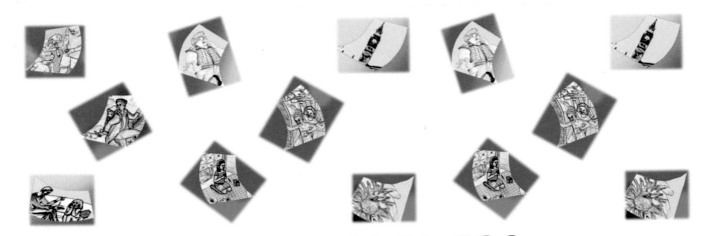

LIVE FEARLESS
SHARE LOVE
HELP OTHERS
GO BOLD
ALWAYS ADVENTUROUS
STAY HOPEFUL
HAVE FAITH
BE BRAVE
FANTABULOUS YOU

Made in the USA
Middletown, DE
19 November 2018